For Justin—
Because our hearts make the best music together.
—J. K.

For all those brave enough to beat their own drum.
Your band will find you.
—J. B.

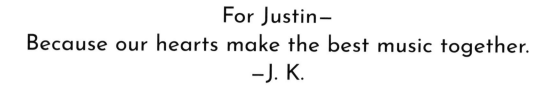

BLOOMSBURY CHILDREN'S BOOKS
Bloomsbury Publishing Inc., part of Bloomsbury Publishing Plc
1385 Broadway, New York, NY 10018

BLOOMSBURY, BLOOMSBURY CHILDREN'S BOOKS, and the Diana logo are trademarks of Bloomsbury Publishing Plc

First published in the United States of America in February 2022
by Bloomsbury Children's Books

Text copyright © 2022 by Jessica Kulekjian
Illustrations copyright © 2022 by Jennifer Bower

Bloomsbury books may be purchased for business or promotional use. For information on bulk purchases
please contact Macmillan Corporate and Premium Sales Department at specialmarkets@macmillan.com

Library of Congress Cataloging-in-Publication Data
Names: Kulekjian, Jessica, author. | Bower, Jennifer, illustrator.
Title: First notes of spring / by Jessica Kulekjian ; illustrated by Jennifer Bower.
Description: New York : Bloomsbury, 2022.
Summary: Forest animals stirring from their winter homes and hibernation
make a variety of noises to welcome spring.
Identifiers: LCCN 2021026245 (print) | LCCN 2021026246 (e-book)
ISBN 978-1-5476-0473-9 (hardcover) • ISBN 978-1-5476-0474-6 (e-book) • ISBN 978-1-5476-0475-3 (e-PDF)
Subjects: CYAC: Spring—Fiction. | Forest animals—Fiction.
Classification: LCC PZ7.1.K84632 Fi 2022 (print) | LCC PZ7.1.K84632 (e-book) | DDC [E]—dc23
LC record available at https://lccn.loc.gov/2021026245

The illustrations were created with pencil and Adobe Photoshop • Typeset in Josefin Sans • Book design by John Candell
Printed in China by Leo Paper Products, Heshan, Guangdong
2 4 6 8 10 9 7 5 3 1

To find out more about our authors and books visit www.bloomsbury.com and sign up for our newsletters.

First Notes of Spring

JESSICA KULEKJIAN

illustrated by
JENNIFER BOWER

BLOOMSBURY
CHILDREN'S BOOKS
NEW YORK LONDON OXFORD NEW DELHI SYDNEY

Every year, after many months of cold and snow, the First Notes of Spring musicians melted winter away with their melodies.

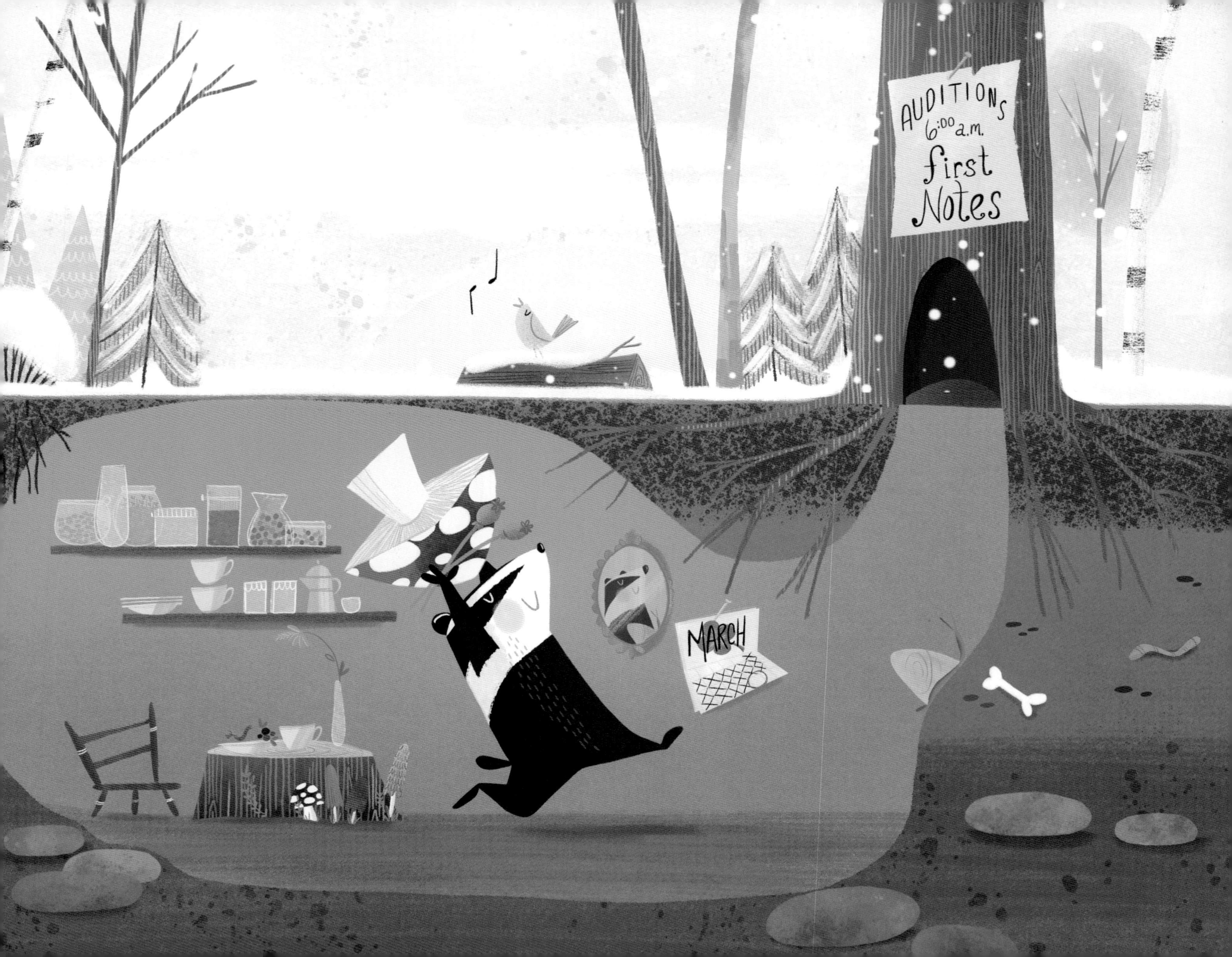
AUDITIONS
6:00 a.m.
first
Notes
MARCH

This year, Juniper was ready
to join them.

With strong sticks, a thumpity toadstool, and
rowdy rhythms, she marched right up to Mr. Moose.
But when she played . . .

BooMey BooM

BOOM!

Mr. Moose plugged his ears, shook his antlers, and groaned, "That's all wrong! You need to sound like *this*."

WHOO whistled the flutes.

Hum Hum sang the strings.

And the little keys played with a *Ringy Ring Ring.*

"I can do that!" said Juniper.

WHOO

Boomey
Boomey!

Hum Hum

Boom
Boom!

Ringy
Ring
Ring

BOOMEY BOOM BOOM!

"Too fast. Too loud. Too WILD!" said Mr. Moose.
"Spring will not bloom to such a ruckus!
Auditions are over!"

DO NOT
DISTURB
REHEARSAL
IN
SESSION

Juniper dragged her drum away.
She had never felt so quiet.

tap-a-tap

"Who's that?"
Juniper tiptoed
forward and found . . .

. . . Holly drumming
on a tree.

"What are you doing?" asked Juniper.
"Looking for bugs," said Holly.

"That's a fun sound. Can I play too?"
Juniper tapped her sticks. "Let's get faster!"

They played together, until they heard
clap-a-clap and found . . .

. . . Darby slapping the ice.
"What are you doing?"
asked Juniper.

"Fixing my fort," said Darby.

"That's a fun sound. Mind if we join?" Juniper clapped her toadstool. "Let's get louder!"

tap-a-tap   clap-a-clap

BOOMEY

BOOM

BOOM!

They paraded through the forest until they heard

thumpity thump

and found . . . .

. . . Dash stomping the ground.
"What are you doing?" asked Juniper.

"Sending messages to my friends," said Dash.

"That sounds fun! Want to play together?"
Juniper hopped and spun. "Let's get wilder!"

Their sound rattled the trees. It shook snow off the branches. It awoke every sleeper inside every den.

Juniper's heart pounded with pride.
"Look what we did!"
Everyone cheered, "We are the
First BEATS of Spring!"

Mr. Moose gasped, "I never knew Spring could wake up with such a bang!" He lowered his antlers.

"The flowers are still sleeping," said Juniper. "We could use some **WHOOS, HUMS,** and **RINGS** to help us wake them."

Juniper led the Beats.

Mr. Moose led the Notes.

And together,
they welcomed Spring.

The Sounds of the Seasons

Juniper's favorite season is spring because it brings a symphony of new beginnings. Ice and snow from the previous winter season *drip-drop* and melt into *rushing* streams and *splashing* puddles. Wildlife *whirls* with activity as animals stir from their winter homes and hibernation, often with young ones by their sides. New flowers *whisper* a welcome to butterflies and bees. Seeds *pop* with fresh beginnings. Birds return and *tweet* sweet songs as the days grow longer. When spring is over, Juniper will have to wait a whole year before her favorite season returns.

Each year, there are four seasons—spring, summer, fall, and winter. They repeat in the same order, over and over again. Why are there seasons? As the Earth spins around the sun, it receives different amounts of sunlight and heat, and these differences create the changes we experience between the warmest and coolest months of the year.

When spring shifts into summer, the longest hours of daylight *buzz* and *hum* with heat and insect sounds. Fall brings *rustling*, cool winds, leaves that change color and drift to *crunch* on the ground. Winter comes with a quiet *hush* of darker days and the coldest temperatures of the year. But after many months of *crackling* cold and snow, spring wakes up again.

What seasonal clues do you notice in your neighborhood? If you made up a spring song, like Juniper, what would it sound like?